In the
Small, Small Pond

For David, still the one.

ISBN 0-590-48119-3

12 11 10   9/9

Printed in the U.S.A.   08

First Scholastic printing, September 1994

In the
Small, Small Pond

Denise Fleming

SCHOLASTIC INC.
New York Toronto London Auckland Sydney

In the small, small

pond...

tadpoles

wriggle

waddle,

wade,

geese parade

hover,

shiver,

wings quiver

drowse, doze,

eyes close

herons
plunge

minnows scatter

circle, swirl,

sweep, swoop,

swallows scoop

claws crack

dabble, dip.

tails

flip

splish,
splash,

paws flash

pile,
pack,

muskrats
stack.

Chill breeze,

winter freeze...

cold night,

sleep tight,

small, small

pond.